For Aunt Sara and Uncle Mike

G. P. PUTNAM'S SONS
A division of Penguin Young Readers Group.
Published by The Penguin Group.
Penguin Group (USA) Inc., 375 Hudson Street, New York, NY 10014, U.S.A.
Penguin Group (Canada), 90 Eglinton Avenue East, Suite 700, Toronto, Ontario M4P 2Y3, Canada
(a division of Pearson Penguin Canada Inc.).
Penguin Books Ltd, 80 Strand, London WC2R 0RL, England.
Penguin Ireland, 25 St. Stephen's Green, Dublin 2, Ireland
(a division of Penguin Books Ltd.).
Penguin Group (Australia), 250 Camberwell Road, Camberwell, Victoria 3124, Australia
(a division of Pearson Australia Group Pty Ltd).
Penguin Books India Pvt Ltd, 11 Community Centre, Panchsheel Park, New Delhi - 110 017, India.
Penguin Group (NZ), 67 Apollo Drive, Rosedale, North Shore 0632, New Zealand
(a division of Pearson New Zealand Ltd).
Penguin Books (South Africa) (Pty) Ltd, 24 Sturdee Avenue, Rosebank, Johannesburg 2196, South Africa.
Penguin Books Ltd, Registered Offices: 80 Strand, London WC2R 0RL, England.

Published simultaneously in Canada. Manufactured in China by South China Printing Co. Ltd.
Design by Marikka Tamura. Text set in Apollo.
The art was done in pastels.
Library of Congress Cataloging-in-Publication Data
Isadora, Rachel. Peekaboo bedtime / Rachel Isadora. p. cm.
Summary: A toddler plays peekaboo with parents, grandparents, toys, and the moon while getting ready for bed.
[1. Toddlers—Fiction. 2. Bedtime—Fiction.] I. Title.
PZ7.I763Pb 2008 [E]—dc22 2007034814
ISBN 978-0-399-24384-4
10 9 8 7 6 5 4 3 2 1

Peekaboo Bedtime

RACHEL ISADORA

G. P. Putnam's Sons

Peekaboo! I see...

my grandma
and grandpa

Peekaboo! I see...

the moon

Peekaboo! I see...

my daddy

Peekaboo! I see...

my cat

Peekaboo! I see...

my grandma

Peekaboo! I see...

my puppy

Peekaboo! I see...

my slippers

Peekaboo! I see...

my duck

Peekaboo! I see...

my mommy

Peekaboo! I see...

my
blankie

Peekaboo! I see...

you!